Hannah Giffard was born in London and studied at
the Norwich School of Art and Bristol Polytechnic. Her parents
are both artists, so she was surrounded by art from an early age.
Her follow up to *Red Fox, Red Fox on the Move*, was enthusiastically
reviewed and selected as a Children's Book of the Year. Her other titles
for Frances Lincoln include the Early Days Board Books
and *Is there Room on the Bus?*, written by Helen Piers.

RED FOX

To Keith, Luke and Joe
with love

First published in Great Britain in 1991 by
Frances Lincoln Limited, 4 Torriano Mews
Torriano Avenue, London NW5 2RZ

First paperback edition 1992

British Library Cataloguing in Publication Data
available on request

ISBN 0-7112-0641-4 hardback
ISBN 0-7112-0747-X paperback

Set in Optima
Printed in Hong Kong

3 5 7 9 8 6 4

RED FOX

◆ Hannah Giffard ◆

FRANCES LINCOLN

The sky darkened as the sun set over the faraway hills.
Red Fox got up from his warm bed inside the den
and stretched. Rose, Red Fox's wife, woke up more slowly.
She had slept all day but she still felt tired. Tired and hungry.

"Stay here and rest," Red Fox told her. "I'll find us something special to eat."
Then he slipped out into the dusk.

Red Fox headed for the farm. "There are always fat chickens in Farmer Bog's yard," he told himself.
He trotted into the yard and stopped suddenly.

A large and very angry guard dog faced him – not at all
what a Red Fox likes to meet.

Red Fox ran off towards the pond, leaving the barking dog pulling at its chain. "There are always juicy green frogs in the reeds," he said to himself.

But tonight there were only tadpoles and an eel — not at all what a Red Fox likes to eat.

He heard a faint rustling in the cornfield nearby.
Could it be a fieldmouse?

But when he parted the tall green wheat there were only
grasshoppers and crickets – not at all what a Red Fox
likes to eat.

The sky was black behind the glowing moon and Red Fox was beginning to wonder if he'd lost his touch. It never took this long to find supper when Rose was with him. Then he heard a scuffling at the edge of the wood . . .

His ears pricked up and he sprang towards the noise. Out of the trees popped a hare. He ran like a wind across the fields. Red Fox chased him down to the railway line.

He was almost close enough to touch the hare when a
fast train came round the bend, surprising Red Fox.

The hare took his chance, and raced up the bank.
Red Fox had lost him.

Tired and thirsty, and wondering if he deserved to be
called a fox at all, Red Fox went to the river for a drink.
He dipped his nose in the cool water, and as he drank
he was amazed to see lights in the water. They were
reflections from the nearby town.

Red Fox had never been to the town before. He had always
been too frightened. But tonight he was desperate.

The huge buildings
seemed to hang in
the sky above him.
He moved through
the streets, hiding
in the shadows.

Red Fox turned a corner and found himself in a narrow street.
Across a yard he saw a woman in a spotted nightgown.

She hummed a tune as she threw a large parcel into the dustbin.
Red Fox's nose began to twitch. What a glorious smell!

Red Fox nudged the lid off the dustbin. Then he jumped right inside. In no time at all he was racing home with the parcel in his mouth.

As he hurried across the fields the sun shone its first beams of the day.

Red Fox entered
the dark den.
Then he paused.
He could hear
squeaking
and
scuffling.

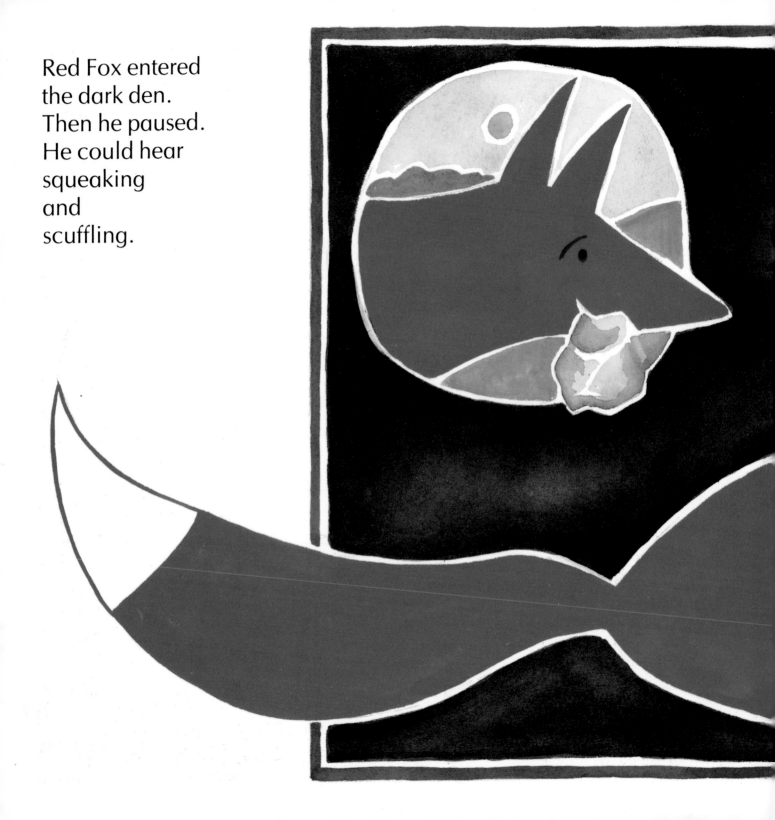

As his eyes got used to the dark he saw five little fox cubs
lying next to Rose.
Red Fox laid his parcel down beside her.

Out rolled some burgers and chips.
"Oh, Red Fox. Aren't you clever!" said Rose smiling.
And together they ate every last piece.

Then, after supper, the new fox family curled up
and slept until a new dusk.

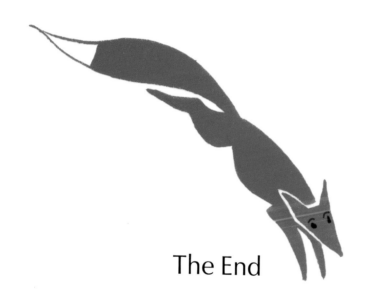

The End

MORE PICTURE BOOKS IN PAPERBACK
FROM FRANCES LINCOLN

RED FOX ON THE MOVE
Hannah Giffard

When a bulldozer tears apart the den of Red Fox and his family, they find themselves on the move. In their search for a new home, they encounter an angry snake and an owl. Finally, after taking refuge on a barge, they wake up in the city, where they find their perfect hole in a beautiful wild garden.

'A truly handsome, original book in wonderful rich colours.' *Books for Children*

Suitable for National Curriculum English - Reading, Key Stage 1
Scottish Guidelines English Language - Reading, Levels A and B

ISBN 0-7112-0819-0   £3.99

DOWN BY THE POND
Margrit Cruickshank
Illustrated by Dave Saunders

Fox thinks he can slink through the farmyard without being noticed. But the cow, the pig and all the other animals catch a glimpse of him, and in a glorious hullabaloo, they soon show who's in charge. A medley of animal noises and a twist in the tale make this rhyming story, with its amusing illustrations and die-cut pages, a delight for all young readers.

Suitable for National Curriculum English - Reading, Key Stage 1
Scottish Guidelines English Language - Reading, Levels A and B

ISBN 0-7112-0978-2   £4.99

FIDDLE-I-FEE
Jakki Wood

An exuberant retelling of a well-known nursery rhyme that will have children singing along in no time. Margaret Lion has arranged the accompanying melody, based on a traditional folk song, for piano and guitar.

Suitable for National Curriculum English - Reading, Key Stage 1
Scottish Guidelines English Language - Reading, Level A

ISBN 0-7112-0860-3   £3.99

Frances Lincoln titles are available from all good bookshops.

Prices are correct at time of printing, but may be subject to change.